RED RARK

GREEN GROOBS

WHITE WIGGLIE

YELLOW YOPP

PINK POG

PARP

RAINBOW RUFF

KNOCK KNOCK
ALIEN

KNOCK
KNOCK

Caryl Hart & Nick East

HODDER CHILDREN'S BOOKS

First published in Great Britain in 2019 by Hodder and Stoughton

Text © Caryl Hart 2019
Illustrations © Nick East 2019

The moral rights of the author and illustrator have been asserted.

A CIP catalogue record of this book
is available from the British Library.

HB ISBN: 978 1 444 93873 9
PB ISBN: 978 1 444 93874 6

10 9 8 7 6 5 4 3 2 1

Printed and bound in China.

FSC
MIX
Paper from
responsible sources
FSC® C104740
www.fsc.org

Hodder Children's Books
An imprint of
Hachette Children's Group
Part of Hodder and Stoughton
Carmelite House
50 Victoria Embankment
London EC4Y 0DZ

An Hachette UK Company
www.hachette.co.uk

www.hachettechildrens.co.uk

Hodder
Children's
Books

KNOCK KNOCK
ALIEN

Caryl Hart & Nick East

KNOCK KNOCK!

Who's at the door?

ONE thing I've never seen before...

"Are you an ALIEN?" I say.
"From far across the Milky Way?
Are you lonely? Are you lost?
How many galaxies have you crossed?"

The creature points
at Granny's chair.
Yikes! TWO blue
Bargles sit right there!

"Oh no!" I gasp.
"Don't wake my gran.
Get down! Be quiet
as you can!"

CREAK

BING

SWOOOSH

BOING

Next, THREE pink Pogs
with stripy lips
bounce through the doorway,
doing flips.

Then FOUR red Rarks with hairy ears
all beam inside to whoops and cheers.

"We must get home," the Bargles say.
"Quick! Start the countdown, right away!"
"Hey, wait!" I call. "What's going on?
What countdown? Stop. You've got it wrong!"

FIVE green Groobs on a sonic broom
grab gadgets from around the room.
They press a button, red and round.
I hear a dreadful wrenching sound.
"At last!" they cry. "Let's leave this place!"

Then . . .

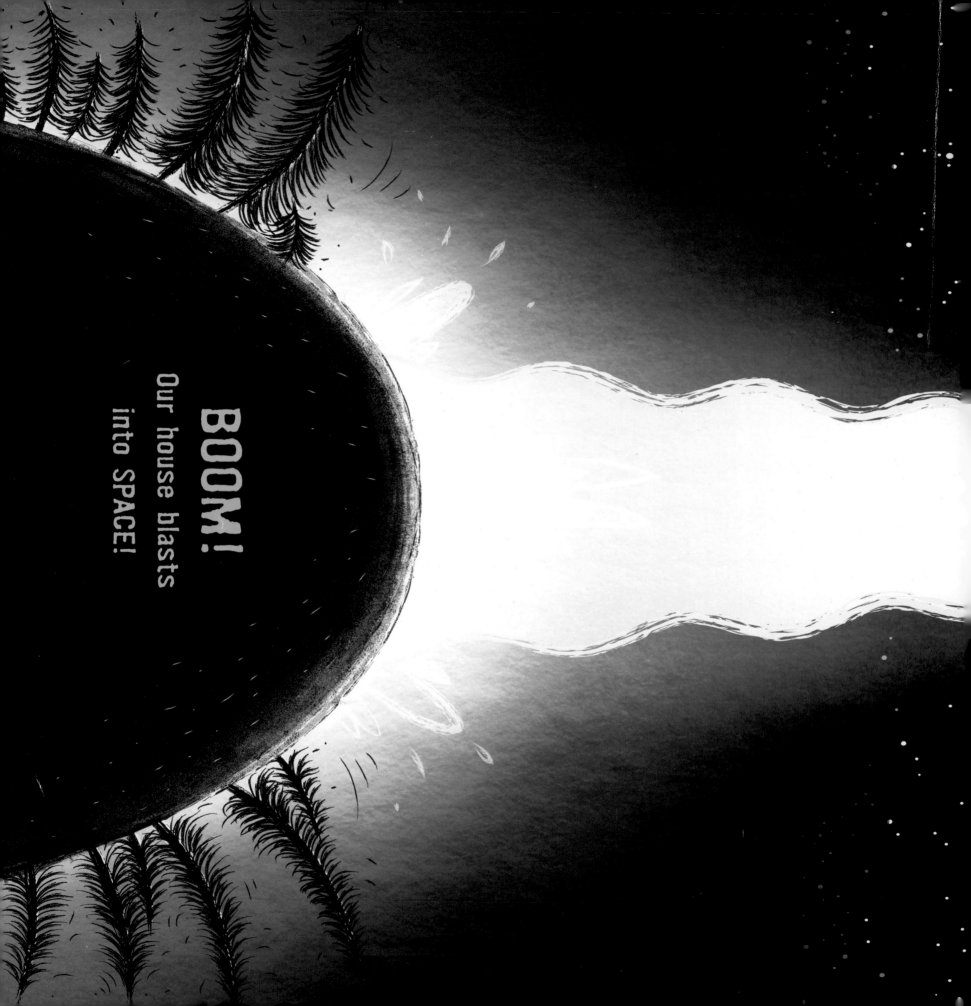

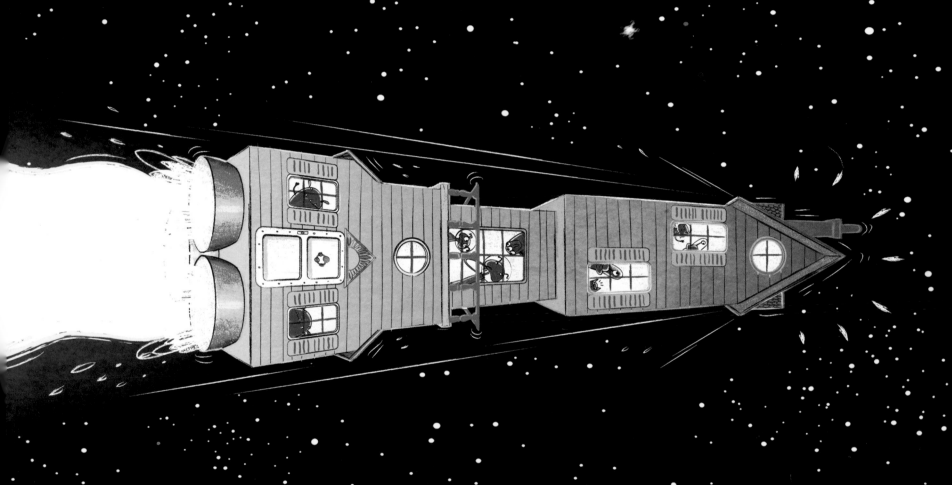

The thrusters ROAR, then fizzle out.
Then Woooah things start to float about!

"Hey, everybody, look at me!
It's fun in zero gravity!"

We zoom off at the speed of light.
But SIX black Buffs bark, "That's not right!
We want to go to Planet Boot.
We'll have to take a faster route."

They grab at the remote control
and steer us through a big black hole!

The black hole twists us inside out
then SNAPs us back and...

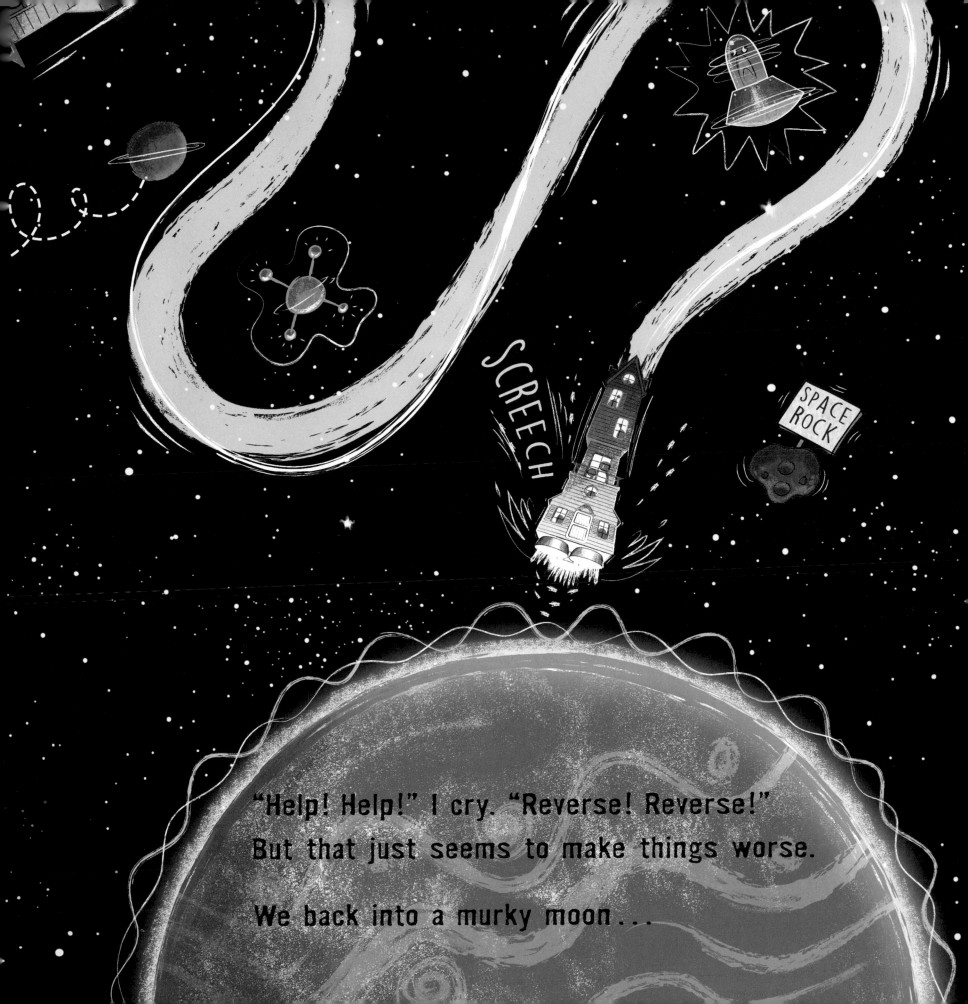

SCREECH

SPACE ROCK

"Help! Help!" I cry. "Reverse! Reverse!"
But that just seems to make things worse.

We back into a murky moon...

... and crash-land in
the swampy gloom.

"Oh dear," I groan. "What shall we do?"
But from the marshes, two by two,
EIGHT slimy purple Pom-Pigs yelp,
"We saw you crash. We'll help, we'll help!"

They fire their lasers down the halls,
to solder all the damaged walls.
NINE yellow Yopps with orange chins
repair our lights and mend our fins.

The Bargles cheer, "Hooray! Hooray!
You've all helped out so much today.
Come home with us, there's lots of room!"
So in they climb and off we

ZOOOM!

PLANET
BOOT

At last we land on Planet Boot.
TEN rainbow Ruffs play pipes. TOOT! TOOT!
"Phew wee," I say. "Wow, what a flight!"
We party long into the night.

At last I say, "I'd better go.
My gran will wake up soon, you know."
My alien buddy hugs me tight.
"Go safely on your homeward flight."

I set the switches, knobs and dials
to Earth...one hundred thousand miles.
Then point the house towards the sky
as all my new friends wave goodbye.

We whizz past comets,
moons and stars,
round Saturn, Jupiter and Mars.
I see the Earth! I see our town!
Then CRUNCH! Our house lands UPSIDE DOWN.

My gran wakes up. "Ohh! What was that?
I've lost my knitting. Where's the cat?"
She takes a look around the place,
then laughs. "I dreamt we were in space!

It seemed quite real just for a while..."

"You must have nodded off," I smile.